STERLING CHILDREN'S BOOKS
New York

An Imprint of Sterling Publishing Co., Inc.
1166 Avenue of the Americas
New York, NY 10036

ISBN 978-1-4027-8339-5

Distributed in Canada by Sterling Publishing Co., Inc.
c/o Canadian Manda Group, 664 Annette Street
Toronto, Ontario, Canada M6S 2C8
Distributed in the United Kingdom by GMC Distribution Services
Castle Place, 166 High Street, Lewes, East Sussex, England BN7 1XU
Distributed in Australia by NewSouth Books
45 Beach Street, Coogee, NSW 2034, Australia

For information about custom editions, special sales, and premium and corporate
purchases, please contact Sterling Special Sales at 800-805-5489
or specialsales@sterlingpublishing.com.

Manufactured in China

Lot #:
4 6 8 10 9 7 5
08/17

sterlingpublishing.com

Design by Jennifer Browning

Robin Hood

Told by Deanna McFadden
Illustrated by Marcos Calo

Robin Hood was an outlaw who lived in Sherwood Forest, near the city of Nottingham.

Nottingham had a wicked sheriff who hated Robin Hood and who was always trying to catch him. The sheriff ruled harshly over his city. He was very rich, but he stole from the poor.

One day, the sheriff of Nottingham and some of the King's Men were bragging about the money they had just stolen from a poor family.

Nearby, Robin Hood heard them talking and yelled, "What you have done is wrong!"

The men just laughed. Robin Hood said, "See that tree way over there? If I can shoot it on my first try, you must give me what you have stolen from the people of my city."

With a single arrow, Robin hit the mark.

The king's archer laughed
even harder.

"Young man," he said, "you cannot
challenge the King's Men! This is
our money now. You cannot have it."

He shot an arrow that barely missed
Robin's head. Robin jumped, then
said, "You are not honest men."

Then Robin Hood let an arrow fly.
It caught the archer's cap, sending it
straight into a tree trunk.

"You have just shot at the king's
archer!" said the sheriff of
Nottingham. "We will make sure
you are punished."

Robin Hood grabbed the stolen money and ran away. From that day forward, he hid deep in Sherwood Forest.

The sheriff of Nottingham told the king about Robin Hood. Of course, the sheriff didn't mention that the archer shot first or that he and the King's Men had stolen from the poor. The king declared Robin Hood an outlaw and offered a reward for his capture. The sheriff promised to find him.

Robin Hood wasn't alone in Sherwood Forest for long. He soon found other outlaws hiding in the woods. They decided to work together and they called themselves the Merry Men.

Robin Hood and the Merry Men were kind and goodhearted, even though they were outlaws. They often disguised themselves, took food and money that the sheriff of Nottingham and the King's Men had stolen, and gave it back to the rightful owners.

One day, Little John, who was
Robin Hood's right-hand man,
ran into camp.

"The king is coming to Nottingham!"
he shouted. "The sheriff has
announced a contest to find the best
archer in England. The prize is a
golden arrow!"

"It's a trap," said Will, another of the Merry Men. "The sheriff is playing a trick to catch dear Robin."

Robin Hood said, "We will enter this archery contest and win! But we must disguise ourselves as tinkers, tailors, and friars. No one must recognize us."

Robin Hood and his men arrived at the contest. The king and queen were there. The benches were filled with lords and ladies of the land. Robin was right—no one recognized them in disguise!

Robin shot his arrow perfectly in every round and won the contest against all the other archers. Afterward there was a grand ceremony, and the sheriff of Nottingham presented him with a golden arrow.

As he was leaving, Robin Hood
pulled off his hat, held up his prize,
and shouted, "I am Robin Hood.
Many thanks to you, Sheriff!" The
crowd gasped. Before disappearing
into Sherwood Forest, he handed
the golden arrow to a poor boy in
the crowd.

The king noticed that Robin Hood gave away his valuable prize. *Robin Hood doesn't seem like an outlaw*, the king thought to himself. He decided to find out.

The next day, the king went into Sherwood Forest disguised as a peasant. He searched and found the Merry Men by their campfire.

"What-ho!" he called out.

"What-ho, to you, good friend," Robin Hood replied. "Come, warm yourself by the fire. Rest your weary bones."

The king joined them. While they talked, he asked how the Merry Men ended up living in Sherwood Forest as outlaws. They all told their stories to the visitor.

Robin Hood spoke last. The king realized that Robin was an honest man and not an outlaw. He removed his disguise and pardoned Robin Hood.

"I trust you all," the king said to the band of Merry Men. "You will be my new sheriff, Robin Hood. Form a band of King's Men and do good work in all parts of my kingdom."

From then on, Robin Hood and his Merry Men were known as King's Men. They were able to help even more people than before. Stories of their bravery and kindness spread throughout the land, and their legend lives on to this day.